This edition first published in 2001 by
Cat's Whiskers
96 Leonard Street, London EC2A 4XD

Cat's Whiskers Australia
56 O'Riordan Street, Alexandria NSW 2015

ISBN 1 903012 52 X

A CIP catalogue record for this book is
available from the British Library

Printed in France by Pollina - n° L84414

ANNE GUTMAN • GEORG HALLENSLEBEN

Lily's Bad Dream

CAT'S Whiskers

THE WATTS PUBLISHING GROUP LTD

I watched a film at my grandma's house. It was about a giant wolf who liked to eat children. "There aren't any giant wolves near here," I kept telling myself all the way home.

Even so, I walked as quickly as I could.

That night, I had a **horrible** dream.

My mother tucked me back into bed.
She sang to me and left the light on.

But I **still** dreamed about the giant wolf.

At school I told George all about it.
He looked very serious and said there
was no such thing as **giant wolves**.
But he offered to come and sleep
at my house if I wanted protection.

That evening I asked my father:
"Do you **really** believe there aren't any wolves here?"
He patted my head in that annoying way of his,
and called to my big sister Anna.

Anna made fun of me. She pretended to look for the wolf everywhere, even inside my favourite red box.

Afterwards she treated me like a baby and told me not to worry. Besides, she said, no wolf would want to **eat me**: I was far too **skinny**.

But that night the dreams were
even **MORE** horrible.

4 My **toy monkey** above the **door**...

5 ...to **scare** him to death...

6 ...when it **drops** on his head?

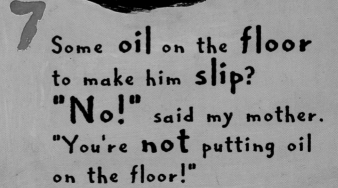

7 Some **oil** on the **floor** to make him **slip**? **"No!"** said my mother. **"You're not** putting oil on the floor!"

But despite everything,
DISASTER!
That night the wolf
came back.

The next day Anna lost her fourth tooth.
To celebrate we all went to the zoo.
My father invited George, too.

George ran around like a mad thing: he wanted
to see every single animal before the zoo closed.

As for me, I watched giraffes, an otter and some monkeys.
And then I found myself by this **big** cage.
As I got closer, I could see
what was written on the sign: WOLF.

...or, at least, no nastier than Mrs Taylor's dog, Alfred. He even looked a bit like Alfred, but with **longer legs.**

I stayed with the wolf for a **long time**.
I was there so long that George fell asleep
and Anna went very quiet.
She wanted to go to the toilet.
I gave the wolf a name. I called him **Snowy**.

That way, the next time I go to see him,
as soon as I call him...

...he'll know that it's ME!